The Right Chord

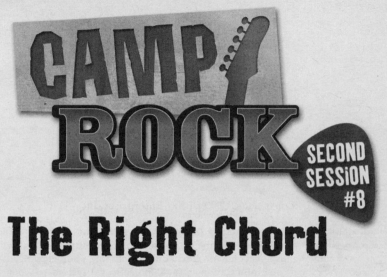

The Right Chord

By James Ponti

Based on "Camp Rock," Written by Karin Gist & Regina Hicks and Julie Brown & Paul Brown

DISNEP PRESS

New York

Printed in the United States of America

First Edition
1 3 5 7 9 10 8 6 4 2

Library of Congress Catalog Card Number on file.
ISBN 978-1-4231-1778-0

For more Disney Press fun, visit www.disneybooks.com
Visit DisneyChannel.com

CHAPTER ONE

For as long as she could remember, Mitchie Torres dreamed of being a performing artist like the ones she saw on the TV shows on *Hot Tunes*. And for as long as she could remember, that dream seemed like a far-fetched fantasy. But at the start of summer, her mother did an amazing thing. Connie Torres got a job as the cook at Camp Rock, making it possible for Mitchie to go where she could eat, drink, and live music twenty-four hours a day.

Now, on the last day of camp, the fantasy no longer seemed so far-fetched. Mitchie was about to sing a duet in the Parents Concert with Colby Miller, one of her new friends from camp.

As was traditional, the Parents Concert was the last one of the summer. It was a chance for the campers to show their parents what they had learned. For Mitchie it was a chance to show her mother how much all of this had meant to her. Right before the song started, she looked out into the audience and saw Mrs. Torres. They both smiled.

The music began, and Mitchie and Colby felt it from their fingers to their toes. The mood of the evening flowed into the song, and when Mitchie held the final note as the music trailed off, the entire audience jumped to their feet and gave them a standing ovation.

"You were great!" Colby cried.

"So were you," Mitchie said, grinning. "You nailed those high notes."

As they smiled and waved at the still-applauding audience, Mitchie was filled with excitement about their performance. But she felt a twinge of sadness because it was all coming to an end.

"I don't know about you," Colby said, leaning over so she could hear him during the applause. "But I need some water. It's hot up here."

Mitchie was hot and thirsty, too, but she didn't want to leave the stage yet. She closed her eyes and tried to freeze this moment in her memory. She wanted to remember exactly how it felt. After a couple seconds she opened her eyes, turned to Colby, and nodded.

"I'm thirsty, too. Let's get out of here."

They waved to the crowd one last time and headed backstage as the next act was coming on.

The first person to greet them was Shane Gray, who gave Colby a high five and then locked eyes with Mitchie.

"Your voice is amazing," he said. "That's the only word for it. Amazing."

Something about Shane's eyes made Mitchie forget how hot and thirsty she was. Those eyes also made her forget about the noise and all the other people who were around them. She imagined that as the lead singer of the superfamous band Connect Three, his eyes did that to a lot of girls. Still . . . he was her friend and that meant a lot.

"Thanks!" she managed to reply as she tried to catch her breath.

It was only a matter of seconds before Caitlyn Gellar, Mitchie's best friend, was there, too, with bottles of ice-cold water. She tossed one to Colby, who instantly started chugging it.

Caitlyn gave her review in a single word. Actually there were four words, but she said them so fast they seemed like one. "Absolutely-unbelievably-incredibly-awesome!"

Mitchie laughed and took a gulp of water. She couldn't believe that all of this had become a part of her life. Before the summer started, she had been a shy kid who wrote songs in secret because she didn't think they were good enough for others to hear. And now she was sharing them with dozens of friends . . . and strangers. Life couldn't get sweeter.

Thirty minutes later, the concert was over and everyone was enjoying a big barbecue down by the lake. Mitchie felt caught in a whirlwind. There were parents to meet and then one by one the good-byes started as friends loaded up their stuff and headed for home.

There were lots of hugs and more than a few tears. People swapped e-mail addresses and promised to keep in touch, but Mitchie didn't know what the future might hold. This was her first time at camp, and it was all new to her. It had been the most amazing time in her life, but now it was coming to an end. Part of her was worried that when she drove away from camp, everything would go back to the way it had been before.

"Well, that's that," the camp director, Brown Cesario, said as the last car pulled away. "I guess that just leaves my super-duper cleanup crew."

He was addressing the small group of campers who were staying for a few extra days to help clean up the camp and get it ready for the long off-season.

Together they were going to get everything spotless, boxed, and loaded for storage. Originally, it was supposed to be just a four-person job, for Mitchie, Shane, Colby, and Lorraine Burgess, who were all technically part of the camp staff.

Shane was a counselor and Brown's

nephew. That meant he had to do whatever his uncle told him. His job was to make sure the cabins were all cleaned out.

Mitchie, Lorraine, and Colby had all worked part-time over the summer in order to attend camp at a discounted rate. Mitchie had helped her mother in the kitchen, while Lorraine oversaw the care and creation of costumes. Colby had asked to help with the maintenance of the musical instruments to cut the cost of his tuition. Any little savings would make his father feel better about the fact that Colby was at a music camp, not home helping him with his boat business.

The foursome had grown to six when some last-minute developments added Tess Tyler and Caitlyn to the cleanup crew.

Tess's mother was T. J. Tyler, a big-time pop star currently in the middle of her North American tour. T. J. had planned it so that she had a few days off to pick up Tess. But according to Tess, she had been held up doing some unscheduled publicity in New York. That meant Tess was going to be doing manual labor for the first time in her life.

Caitlyn's parents were also stuck on tour, although theirs wasn't nearly as glamorous. They had spent the summer driving an RV around the country and it had broken down outside of Yellowstone National Park. It took them a couple of days to get it fixed, and now they were behind schedule.

"All right, everyone!" Brown said, calling the group to order. "This is the part where I remind you that camp is over. That means we have a few days of hard work ahead of us."

The six of them groaned.

"But that doesn't mean we aren't going to have some fun," he added.

"Yeah," Mitchie joked. "It's *so* much fun scrubbing pots and pans."

"Don't forget cleaning out bathrooms," Caitlyn interjected. "The bathrooms are tons of fun."

Mitchie smiled as, out of the corner of her eye, she saw Tess shudder at the thought of cleaning out a bathroom.

"Yeah, yeah," Brown said. "I know it's a drag, but I have a deal for you."

"What kind of deal?" Shane asked.

"I'm thinking of adding one more concert to our little summer schedule."

"That sounds like an interesting deal," Mitchie said hopefully. Even though she had been onstage just a few hours earlier, she was already missing the feeling.

Brown thought about it for a moment. "We've got three days to get this place clean. But we've added two workers. If I've done my math correctly, I'm thinking with the extra help we can have it all done in two. If you can do that, we can put on a concert on the third day."

"We can *definitely* do that," Lorraine said.

Brown smiled. He had come up with this on the spot, so it was nice to get such a warm reception. "But," he warned, "it's not going to be a jam or any sort of competition. We've had enough of those. I want this to be a little different. This show is just going to be *about* the music."

Suddenly, this sounded a bit suspicious.

"I'm going to give each of you a specific era in rock and roll, and during the next few days you're going to learn as much as you can about it."

"You mean in between scrubbing the pots and pans and cleaning the bathrooms?" Caitlyn said.

"Exactly," Brown said with a laugh. "Then at the special concert, you're going to perform a song from your assigned era."

"That sounds kind of cool," Mitchie commented, nodding.

"And in return," Brown added, "I'm going to have a special surprise for you."

"What kind of special surprise?" Tess asked.

Brown just smiled. "One that's worth it. Believe me."

The six of them shared a look as they considered Brown's idea. It certainly sounded like more fun than cleaning.

"We're in," Shane said, and the others nodded.

"Great!" Brown exclaimed. "This is going to be fantastic. I've got some things to get ready—and you've got a camp to clean."

Brown hurried off toward his cabin while the six of them looked at the mess that had been left after the barbecue. Suddenly, they all realized how much work there was to do.

"Yippee," Colby said, trying to sound enthusiastic.

Mitchie wasn't looking forward to the cleanup anymore than the others. But now there was something special waiting at the end. Much to her delight, Camp Rock wasn't quite over yet.

CHAPTER TWO

Three Days Later . . .

The alarm went off and Mitchie hit the snooze button. Her entire body was sore, and she wanted ten more minutes just to lie perfectly still.

Although she had been dreading the thought of leaving Camp Rock, two solid days of cleaning and scrubbing had made her much more open to the idea. In those two days, a place that had once been filled with music and friends was now one that only inspired visions of brushes, brooms, and aching muscles.

On the other side of the cabin, her best friend and roommate, Caitlyn, was sleeping fitfully. After a summer filled with countless late-night talks about everything from camp to boys to their favorite bands, Caitlyn had become what Mitchie always imagined a sister would be like.

"*Arrrgggh*," Caitlyn said as she snapped awake with a sudden yelp.

"What's the matter?" Mitchie asked, startled.

Caitlyn looked around the room to get her bearings. "I was having another nightmare," she said, her heart still racing.

"What was this one about?"

"A giant bathroom that could never be fully cleaned," she answered, panting. "It was horrible."

Mitchie fought the urge to laugh.

"Well, the bathrooms are all clean now," she assured her. "Come on, it's time to get up."

Caitlyn nodded. "I think I need a long, hot shower."

"Good idea," Mitchie told her.

Caitlyn was still in the shower when Mitchie left the cabin and headed for the Mess Hall of Fame. It felt strange to walk across camp with everything so quiet and empty.

A gust of chilly air blew across the lake, and Mitchie flipped up the collar of her fleece jacket. Summer was definitely ending. She and her mother were leaving for home early the next morning. Soon school would start, and it would be homework and quizzes and . . .

When Mitchie opened the door to the kitchen, the first face she saw was Shane's.

Not a bad way to start the last day, she thought.

"Crikey, it's early," Shane said, speaking in an exaggerated British accent. "How ye doin' on this fine day?"

Mitchie laughed. "I'm, like, totally radical," she replied, trying her best to sound like a surfer girl.

"Is this all part of Brown's big plan?" Mitchie's mom asked as she expertly scrambled some eggs in a skillet.

"Like, totally," Mitchie answered.

Mitchie quickly filled her mother in on the situation. Originally Brown had just wanted each of them to perform a song from a different era of rock and roll. But sometime over the past three days, he'd also decided he wanted them to try to stay in character as much as possible during the final day.

"He says it will make everything more authentic," Shane said, still working on his British accent.

"And you would be?" Connie asked him.

"I'm straight out of the British Invasion of

the sixties. You must have been there—the Rolling Stones, the Who, the Beatles."

"Actually," Connie said as she jokingly gave him the stink-eye, "I'm not quite old enough to have experienced all that first-hand. But of course I've heard their music."

"I'm sorry," Shane said as he flashed a guilty smile and momentarily broke character. "I didn't mean to imply that you were old or anything."

"It's okay," Connie said with a laugh. "I know you guys think anything older than twenty-one is ancient." She turned to her daughter. "And you would be?"

"I'm, like, totally the new wave and pop scene from the early eighties," Mitchie said, twisting a strand of hair around her finger as she talked. "It's *grody* to the max!"

Connie laughed. "*That*, I *did* experience," she said. "That was *my* era. You should have seen me. I had all the clothes. I had all the posters. I even had an autographed picture of Belinda Carlisle. It was epic."

"Wait a second," Mitchie said. "I know that name. Linda Carlisle. I was reading up on new wave bands the other day. What group was she in? Bananarama?"

"As if?" Mrs. Torres responded in perfect eighties slang. "First of all, it's *Be*linda, not Linda. And she was only the lead singer of my favorite group, the Go-Go's."

"That's right, the Go-Go's," Mitchie said, remembering. "I never knew they were your favorite group."

"I saw them in concert three times," Connie added, suddenly bopping to a beat in her head. She scooped the eggs from the skillet onto their plates.

"Thanks," Mitchie said, smiling at her mom's moves. She took a deep breath. "These smell great."

"Actually," Connie corrected. "Back in the day, we would have said they smelled *gnarly*."

"*Gnarly*'s good?" Mitchie asked, perplexed.

Connie nodded. "To the max."

Shane took a bite of egg and smiled as if it was the most delicious thing he'd ever eaten. He started serenading Connie to the tune of the Beatles song "Yesterday."

Scrambled eggs
How I love to eat your scrambled eggs

Mitchie laughed. "What's that supposed to be?"

"Paul McCartney," Shane answered. "When he wrote the song 'Yesterday,' he started with the music. He used the words *scrambled eggs* until he came up with *yesterday*. I learned that from my research. And it also happens to fit this particular occasion."

"That's pretty cool," Mitchie said, impressed. Shane had really done his homework.

In between all the cleaning and packing, they had tried to learn as much as they could about their different eras.

"The more you know about them, the more you understand their music," Brown had told everybody. "And the more you understand their music, the more you understand your own."

Research meant listening to songs and hanging out in the camp library, which was filled with books, classic performance videos, and neatly organized stacks of Brown's music magazines.

In fact, the library had been a key to their survival during cleanup. Whenever they were too tired to continue working, they were allowed to take a break and head there. And, since Brown wanted them to have access to everything, he didn't make them clean out the library. He would take care of it himself.

"What song are you doing tonight?" Mitchie asked Shane as they left the kitchen and walked out into the dining room.

"I still haven't decided," he answered. "It's so hard to settle on one."

"Tell me about it," she answered with a sigh. "Well, we've got until eight o'clock, I guess."

The dining room was empty and all the tables but one had been folded up and pushed against the wall. Mitchie sat down first and smiled when Shane took the seat right next to her.

When the summer started, all Mitchie knew about Shane was what she had seen on *Hot Tunes* or read in the gossip magazines. And almost all of that was negative. According to them, the lead singer of Connect Three was just another spoiled rotten rock star.

Now she knew that despite some well-publicized mistakes, Shane was a terrific guy.

They had become close friends and loved to goof around, talk in-depth about music, and go for the occasional canoe ride. Now she wondered what it was going to be like when she went back to the real world and he returned to superstardom.

A few minutes later, they were joined by Colby. Brown had given him alternative rock and grunge, so he was trying his best to seem deep and thoughtful. At least as deep and thoughtful as he could manage while also eating a breakfast big enough to feed half the grunge bands in Seattle.

"What is all that?" Shane asked in stunned amazement.

"It's my last breakfast with Mrs. Torres," Colby said with a smile as he ran over the menu. "She made me all my favorites. Breakfast burrito, Texas toast and bacon, the hash browns she makes with the little peppers and onions, and orange juice."

"That's unbelievable," Shane responded. "You're not even human."

"Don't listen to him, Colby," Mitchie said. "You have made my mom's summer. She loves cooking for people who appreciate her food so much."

Colby smiled and said something that they

couldn't quite understand because he was chewing a big chunk of Texas toast at the same time.

At that moment, Caitlyn entered from the kitchen, carrying a tray loaded with enough food to rival Colby's. She actually wasn't walking with her tray so much as she was swaggering with it. It was all part of her role. She had been assigned hip-hop and was already fully into character. "Yo, yo, yo, word up!"

"Word," Shane replied as they bumped fists and she sat down.

There was a moment of silence, and then everybody laughed, no one louder than Caitlyn.

There was something kind of funny about little Caitlyn trying to act like an oversize rap personality. But the truth was, Caitlyn loved hip-hop and had been thrilled when Brown assigned it to her.

Tess came in right after Caitlyn carrying a tray containing a bowl of cereal, fresh fruit, and a glass of orange juice. Even though they were indoors and it was summer, Tess was wearing sunglasses and a scarf. The funny thing was that Mitchie couldn't tell if she was in costume or just being Tess.

Colby swallowed a hunk of breakfast burrito and finally came up for air long enough to talk. "How's it going, Miss Thang?"

"That would be Miss Diva," Tess corrected. "A Motown diva, to be exact."

Shane couldn't help but laugh. "That's a stretch."

Mitchie swallowed nervously, not sure how Tess was going to react. But after pretending to have hurt feelings for a moment, Tess flashed a huge smile and rolled her eyes. "I have absolutely *no* idea why Brown picked that for me."

Now they all laughed, and Mitchie sighed with relief. She and Tess had gotten off to a rough start, but things had gotten much better since, and she now considered Tess a friend. At least here at camp. Mitchie wondered if they'd still keep in touch during the school year.

"Where's Lorraine?" Caitlyn asked right before she took a bite out of an apple.

No one had seen her.

Just then Mrs. Torres came in carrying a basket of blueberry muffins and singing something that Mitchie didn't recognize. She assumed it was a Go-Go's song.

"Here you go, guys," Connie said as she put the muffins in the center of the table.

"Muffins, too?" Mitchie asked.

Connie shrugged. "Today's the last day. So I'm cooking whatever we've got left. It's either that or throw it out."

"Heaven," Colby said as he grabbed a muffin and took a bite. "I'm in heaven."

The others shared a look.

"Amazing," Caitlyn said. "He's like an eating machine."

"Mom, have you seen Lorraine?" Mitchie asked.

"She was the first one here this morning," Connie explained. "She wanted me to tell you all that as soon as you were done with breakfast, you should head over to wardrobe. She has a surprise for you."

"I wonder what it is," Colby said.

"Maybe, if you're lucky, it will be more food," Caitlyn joked.

"Nah," Colby said, totally missing the fact that she was kidding. "You know how she is about food around her clothes. Although, I could go for something sweet to hold me over till lunch."

The others just laughed, because they knew that despite the feast he had just consumed, Colby was one hundred percent serious.

CHAPTER THREE

Because she had come to Camp Rock on the later side, Lorraine Burgess was technically considered a "newbie." Despite this, she had a level of respect from the other campers typically reserved for the "vets" who had established their reputations after attending for years.

This reputation had nothing to do with her lovely singing voice or the mad skills she demonstrated on the piano. Those were impressive. But most of the kids at Camp Rock were impressive when it came to music. The trait that made Lorraine stand out was her talent with clothes—Mitchie and Caitlyn called her a *superpower*.

Lorraine was a genius when it came to wardrobe. She could sew, alter, and design like no one any of them had ever seen. More importantly, she saw potential in things that no one else saw. She could take any three random articles of clothing and with a few quick flourishes turn them into a single outfit that was not only cutting-edge, but that also made the pieces seem as if they had been made to go together.

Brown had happily given her total control of what had formerly been known as the Costume Cabin. The first thing she did was rename it the Wardrobe Studio.

"Costumes are for Halloween," she explained. "Performing artists wear wardrobe."

Since then, Lorraine had successfully turned what was once little more than a glorified closet into the centerpiece of the camp. No one—not even Tess Tyler—went onstage without first stopping by for a consultation with Lorraine.

Now, though, they weren't sure why they were coming.

"Look," Colby said as he entered the studio with the others. He held up his hands for inspection. "No candy!"

"Thank you," Lorraine said with a laugh. Colby had a bad habit of eating candy bars during fittings. "Chocolate and white linen simply do not mix," she had told him on more than one occasion.

"What's our surprise?" Mitchie asked excitedly as they all sat down on the wooden benches in the corner of the cabin.

"I know tonight is not officially a jam," Lorraine said. "But it is the last time we will perform together. At least until next summer.

So, I wanted to pick out some items that I thought might come in handy today while we're in character and tonight when we go onstage."

"Like what?" Caitlyn asked with great anticipation.

"Like this," Lorraine said as she pulled out a jacket and handed it to Shane. "For our British invader."

She had taken an old denim jacket and dyed it black. Then she had sewn a British flag onto the back of the jacket and added some red piping to the shoulders and pockets.

"This is amazing," Shane said, slipping it on. "I've never seen anything like it."

"I'm glad you like it," Lorraine said, trying not to smile too much at the compliment. Shane still made her slightly nervous. After all, he was a *rock star*. "If it doesn't fit right, I can adjust the sleeves."

Shane moved his arms around, testing it out. "It's a perfect fit," he said. "Don't change a thing."

"Now, for the queen of hip-hop," Lorraine said, turning to Caitlyn. "I went a little old school."

Caitlyn smiled broadly. "I like old school."

"I found a choice hat and some serious bling."

She gave Caitlyn a black porkpie hat, a thick necklace with a hood ornament hanging from it, and two giant rings that covered three fingers each. One read HIP and the other read HOP.

"This is da bomb," Caitlyn said as she put it all on. She tilted the hat to one side and struck a pose that made her look just like a famous rapper. "How do I look?"

"Awesome," Mitchie said happily with a little clap. "Lorraine, you are the best wardrobe person ever!"

"True dat," Caitlyn added, still trying to keep up the rap talk.

"Thank you," Lorraine said proudly. "But, you're probably just saying that because you know I found you some totally rad gear."

"You did?"

"Of course I did," Lorraine said as she started handing Mitchie the clothing. "Purple stirrup pants, a lime green sweatshirt cut so you can wear it off the shoulder, and this hot pink cowboy hat."

The others stared at the outfit, unsure what to make of it.

"Are you sure about that?" Caitlyn asked in her regular voice. "Those colors don't really . . . go together."

"I know," Lorraine said. "That's why I had Mitchie's mom come down and check it out."

"What did she say?"

"She called it gnarly," Lorraine answered.

"That means it's good," Mitchie explained.

"And trust me," Lorraine added. "When you put it all on together, it works. It defies every law of fashion, but somehow it works."

Mitchie disappeared into one of the changing rooms in back. A few moments later, she came bopping into the room, a dancing blur of vibrant colors.

"What do you think?" she asked.

"Gnarly," Caitlyn said.

"Totally," added the others.

"Got anything for me?" Colby said, flashing a hopeful smile. Then he looked over at Mitchie and shuddered. "Maybe not quite as colorful as what you got her."

"Do not worry," Lorraine said playfully. "You grunge and alt-rock guys typically avoid bright colors."

Colby breathed a sigh of relief.

Lorraine listed the items while she handed them to him one by one. "Flannel shirt, plaid shorts, high-top sneakers and wool cap."

Colby nodded and smiled as he looked down at the armful of clothes he was holding. "Believe me, if I wasn't supposed to be so dark and serious, I'd be jumping up and down and high-fiving you right now."

"I completely understand," she said with a

friendly pat on his shoulder. "I wouldn't want you to fall out of character."

Colby disappeared into a dressing room and returned a minute later looking like he came straight out of Seattle circa 1992.

Now all eyes turned to the one person still remaining.

"Don't even think about it," Tess warned. "I'm not wearing a costume."

"It's not a costume," Lorraine said. "It's wardrobe."

"Whatever you want to call it," Tess said. "This is not a final jam or a concert or anything else. It's just us performing onstage for each other. Believe me, I have plenty of wonderful clothes that will do fine."

Lorraine smiled. After spending the entire session sharing a cabin with Tess, she knew just how to get her intrigued.

"I know. That's why I wasn't going to get you anything. I mean, your clothes are to die for. But then I saw a gown that just screamed

Motown diva. Believe me, it's not a costume. It's more Beyoncé on the cover of *Vogue*."

It was the mention of Beyoncé and *Vogue* that hooked Tess.

"We'll see about that," she said, trying to hide her sudden interest. "I guess, since you went to the trouble, I should at least look at it."

Now it was time to reel her in. Lorraine turned to a rack and unzipped a hanging garment bag to reveal a beautiful black-and-white gown. It looked like it belonged on the red carpet at the Grammys. Even Tess couldn't hide her excitement.

"I love it!" she squealed. "You really are a genius when it comes to wardrobe."

This was such an honest and uncommon compliment from Tess that the others just remained quiet for a moment to let Lorraine enjoy it.

"What about *your* wardrobe for tonight?" Colby asked Lorraine.

"Yeah," Mitchie said. "What do you have picked out for glam rock?"

Now Lorraine was really smiling. "It's special. But, I'm going to spring that on you guys tonight. That's my last surprise."

"I can hardly wait," Caitlyn said.

Just then, the door swung open and in walked Brown. He gave them the once-over, checking out the new outfits.

"I like it," he said. "Tonight should be a good show. But the question is, will it be an amazing 'think about it for the rest of your life' show? Are we going to end on the right chord?

"As soon as you're done with your work," he went on, "I want you to meet me at my cabin. There are musical mysteries that need to be solved."

With that, Brown spun around and left.

They all shared a look, unsure what to make of his cryptic hints. Musical mysteries?

"Knowing Uncle Brown," Shane said, "this could be really great."

"Absolutely," Lorraine agreed. "So let's get busy."

CHAPTER FOUR

"It's like looking at my younger self," Connie said when she saw Mitchie wearing her new-wave outfit. "Lorraine nailed it."

"You wore colors like this all the time?" Mitchie asked.

Connie flashed a big smile. "Every day."

Normally, Mitchie would have changed before working in the kitchen. But they were supposed to stay in character as much as possible during the day. Besides, she wasn't going to be doing any messy food preparation. Most of the appliances and equipment had already been scrubbed clean. Mitchie and Caitlyn were just moving them into Connie's catering truck.

"This truck is so cool," Caitlyn said as she slid the side door open. "It's like a kitchen on wheels."

"It *is* a kitchen on wheels," Mitchie said as she carried a stack of pots onto the vehicle.

Mitchie's parents had turned a delivery truck into the ultimate catering operation. It had a grill, an oven, a small sink, and a microwave. A large skylight in the roof made sure it stayed nice and bright.

There was a wall filled with cabinets and drawers designed to hold specific items. The names of these items were written on the drawers, making it easy to put things away. Mitchie opened the one marked POTS and slid them in. They fit perfectly.

"What do you think Brown meant earlier when he said there were musical mysteries?" Caitlyn asked.

"I have no idea," Mitchie said. "With Brown it could be anything."

While Mitchie and Caitlyn were helping close up the kitchen, Colby and Shane were with Dee La Duke, the camp's music director, doing an inventory of all the musical instruments and equipment.

Colby was used to helping organize the band room back at his school. But he was impressed with how hard Shane was working. Colby had been intimidated by the star when he first came to camp. But now he felt comfortable with everyone. Even Shane.

As they cleaned, they tried to get some info out of Dee on what Brown had been talking about, but it was useless. If she knew anything about Brown's plans, Dee wasn't letting on.

Meanwhile, Lorraine and Tess were working in the Wardrobe Studio. Actually, Lorraine was working while Tess was on her cell phone trying to get in touch with her mother.

At first, Lorraine thought it was very cool that Tess's mom was a pop star. She was even a little bit jealous. But as she observed Tess during the summer, she had seen that there was a definite downside.

Tess always had trouble getting in touch with her mom. And when she did, there was never time for more than a quick hello or e-mail. This made Lorraine appreciate how great it was that her mom was always there for her.

My mom may not be famous, Lorraine thought. But she's a star to me.

"I understand," Tess said into the phone, trying not to sound disappointed. "I'll call again after the photo shoot."

When Tess snapped the phone shut,

Lorraine tried to look busy. They were friendly, but Tess was not one to open up about personal problems or anything that cast her in any light other than the spotlight.

"My mom's doing a cover shoot for *People* magazine," Tess offered. "She hates that kind of stuff."

"Who wouldn't?" Lorraine answered.

Tess nodded absently and quickly changed the subject. The topic was off-limits.

Within an hour, they had all finished their work and were sitting in Brown's cabin. Even Dee and Connie had come along. They all wanted to know what Brown had planned.

Unlike the rest of camp, Brown's cabin hadn't been packed up at all. He was staying on for a few more weeks. Some of his old bandmates were coming by, and they were going to jam.

"Hello, everybody," Brown said as he entered the room. "I want to play a record.

You *do* know what a record is, don't you?"

They all laughed. Brown was always joking about how old and out-of-date he was.

He had a huge record collection that was stored along one side of the room. Reaching over to a shelf, he pulled out an album.

"This is a record album," he said jokingly, pointing to it. "Inside the cover is the sleeve, which protects the record from getting scratched. And inside the sleeve is the actual record."

He held it up for them to see.

They played along and oohed and aahed.

"Back in the days before you could download songs or burn your own CDs, if my mates and I wanted to listen to music we could either turn on the radio or play a record.

"We played them on these," he continued as he placed the large round disk on a turntable. "This, by the way, is called a record player."

They laughed.

He set the needle down on the record, and a moment later music started to play. The first thing Caitlyn noticed was how scratchy it was.

"Who can tell me who this is?" Brown asked.

The campers looked at each other and then collectively shook their heads. It sounded familiar, but they had no idea who was singing.

"I know," Mrs. Torres said gleefully.

Brown smiled. "Please enlighten these uncultured young minds."

"The Beach Boys," Mrs. Torres said. "I had this album."

"Was yours as scratchy as his?" Caitlyn joked.

"It is scratchy," Brown said, "because I played it about ten thousand times. I used to sit in my room and play this album over and over. This was the record that hooked me on rock and roll."

He closed his eyes and listened to the music. For a moment, he felt like he was a kid again back in his room. "Listen to how their voices come together to make one beautiful sound. I was growing up on the other side of the world and somehow these five voices from California spoke right to my heart. It was magic.

"That is why I challenged all of you to learn about music outside of what you already know. You'll be amazed when someone you've never heard of lights you up inside."

Mitchie loved the way Brown talked about music. Most of the music teachers she'd had talked about the way to play an instrument or the importance of practicing. But with Brown it was always deeper. For him music made the world go 'round.

"So let's get started," he said. "Who wants to tell us about their era?"

Mitchie looked around and saw that no one else was jumping up to go first. "Okay, I'll go," she said. "I'm, like, totally into the new-wave sound."

"Great," Brown said. "You've got the lingo down. You're dressed perfectly. But tell me something deeper. Tell me about the music."

Mitchie was stumped. "What do you mean?"

"Tell us anything," Brown said. "There's no wrong answer. You've listened to the music. You've read about it. Tell us anything you've learned."

"Well, I've learned that my mom was really into the Go-Go's."

"I love the Go-Go's, too. They've got great music, but did you know they were the first all-female rock band who wrote their own music to have a number one album? They helped make it possible for you to make your mark in music."

"Wow. I had no idea," Mitchie said. "I just like their sound."

For the next hour Brown led an amazing discussion in which the campers talked about their various eras. Along the way he told them a lot about musical history. He talked about how U2 formed as a band when they were only teenagers. He told them how Stevie Wonder and Ray Charles changed the way the world looked at people who were blind or had other disabilities.

Brown also explained that while dressing in clothes from a certain era or using slang from that time was helpful, it only scratched the surface. The thing that really mattered was the music, the words, the emotions.

"What were the artists saying with their songs? How did they change the way people thought or looked at the world? What did they do musically to create a new sound or to inspire a new way to dance?"

By the time he was done, the campers were brimming with excitement.

"Now for what I lured you here with—the musical mysteries," he said with a smile.

They leaned forward in eager anticipation.

"As you all know," Brown went on, "I've

spent a fair amount of time on the road and have had the good fortune to play alongside some of the greatest acts of all time."

They nodded. Brown had incredible stories about the famous rock stars and bands he'd played with—and a tendency to share them all in great detail.

"And, during that time I've managed to accumulate some interesting pieces of musical history and memorabilia."

Now the group was getting even more excited.

"Tonight, you are going to have a chance to use some of these items when you perform. I'm talking actual items used by some of the biggest stars in music history."

"This is so cool!" Colby exclaimed.

"But first," Brown said with a wave of his hand, "you're going to have to find them. I have hidden them all over the camp."

Their eyes opened wide.

"Here's a map of the entire camp," he said,

laying it out on the table. "And there is a shovel on the porch."

"Shovel?" Caitlyn said. "Did you bury this stuff?"

"Maybe," Brown said with a sly smile. "That's for you to figure out."

"How?" asked Mitchie.

"I have a clue and a poem for each of you," he said. "If you've studied—if you can get past the clothes and the slang and try to understand the music—you'll be able to find the artifacts."

"And if we don't?" Caitlyn asked with a gulp.

"Then we'll have a *fine* show tonight," he said. "Not an amazing 'think about it for the rest of your life' kind of show. But a fine one."

They all let this sink in for a moment.

"I vote for the one we'll never forget," Colby said.

"Absolutely," replied Shane. "What are we waiting for? Let's start looking!"

CHAPTER FIVE

Brown laid six manila envelopes on the table, one for each of them. He wished everyone luck and left with Dee and Connie.

The campers didn't hesitate. They grabbed their envelopes and set out, determined to solve their mysteries and unearth a piece of rock-and-roll history.

Caitlyn, who loved puzzles, was so excited that she started to giggle. She found a spot at a picnic table and set her envelope down in front of her. CAITLYN—HIP-HOP was written in marker across the front.

Brown had given her hip-hop because she wanted to be a producer and so much of a rap song's success depended on its producer. He told her hip-hop was one of the first musical styles completely created in America since jazz, and he challenged her to be inventive in her research.

He got her listening to some early rappers, and she liked the way they took parts of existing songs, such as a drumbeat or a guitar riff, and turned them into something new. It was the kind of thing she liked to do when she was playing around with her instruments.

She opened the envelope and pulled out two pieces of paper. The first was a poem entitled "Recipe for Rap."

A rap producer is a special fixer,
An artist who controls the mixer

To blend the parts and make them cook
And bake a sound that's off the hook.

Caitlyn smiled as she read the poem. Brown was nothing if not creative. She read it again and giggled.

Then she pulled out the other piece of paper. It was sheet music filled in with musical notes. Across the top of it, Brown had written the word *produce*. Caitlyn nodded. She obviously needed to produce a recording of the music. But when she looked at the sheet again, she crinkled up her nose in confusion. The music wasn't really music at all. It was just practice scales.

"You want me to produce scales?" she said aloud as if Brown were there with her.

She turned over the paper to make sure there were no other clues written on the back. There weren't. She quickly realized this was not going to be as easy as she had first thought. She reread the poem once more and thought about it. As far as she could figure, she was supposed to produce a recording of scales. Maybe add a hip-hop beat to it or something. Hopefully, if she did that she might figure out what the clue actually meant.

It wasn't much of a plan, but at least it was something. And she was glad she had an excuse to go to the recording studio. It was her favorite place at camp. It's where she liked to experiment with different techniques and where she and Mitchie had come up with some great songs.

When she got to the studio, she found Colby digging around in one of the closets.

"Find your treasure yet?" Caitlyn asked.

"Just getting a guitar," he said as he pulled out a case and set it on the table. "We stored a couple of acoustics in here last night."

"Let me guess," Caitlyn said with a smile. "Brown gave you a piece of music?"

Colby held the sheet music up in the air. "How'd you know?"

"I got some, too," she said, holding hers up. "Only mine's not really music. They're just scales."

"Hmmm," Colby said with a nod. "I don't know what mine is. Brown very helpfully crossed out the name of the song. Hopefully, I'll recognize it when I play it."

Colby placed the sheet music on a stand and started to play it on his guitar.

"That's so familiar," he said, missing a few notes as he warmed up, but quickly getting the hang of it.

"Keep playing," Caitlyn said. "I know that song. It's on the tip of my tongue."

Colby nodded and kept playing.

Finally, it came to Caitlyn. She laughed. A lot. "That is so like Brown."

"What?" Colby asked, still not able to identify it. "What song is it?"

"Keep going," she replied. "I'll sing it for you."

Colby kept playing, and when he reached the chorus, Caitlyn sang along. It was the classic U2 song, "I Still Haven't Found What I'm Looking For."

Colby stopped playing and shook his head. "Very funny, Brown." Then he started laughing. "Well, I guess I'll just have to keep looking until I find what I'm looking for. I just don't know where to begin."

"Did he give you a poem?" Caitlyn asked.

Colby nodded. "Oh, yeah. It was really helpful, too," he said sarcastically. Pulling a sheet of paper out of his envelope, he read "The Edge of Music" to Caitlyn.

"Alt rockers and grunge musicians
Are just like old-time magicians
With tricks so hard to believe
Like the one hidden up Paul David
    Hewson's sleeve."

Caitlyn thought about it for a moment and

then shook her head. "I got nothing."

Colby laughed. "Welcome to the club. Because that's what I've got, too."

"Who's Paul David Hewson?" she asked.

"I wish I knew," he replied. "And more importantly, I wish I knew where his sleeve was."

Caitlyn mulled this over for a moment and then had an idea. She snapped her fingers and pointed. "I bet it's in wardrobe!"

Colby slapped the table. "Why didn't I think of that? It makes so much sense."

In a flash, Colby bolted out of the recording studio and headed for the wardrobe cabin. "Good luck," he called cheerfully over his shoulder.

"Thanks," Caitlyn said. "You, too."

In his mad dash across the camp, Colby slipped twice, plopped into the middle of a mud puddle, and almost ran into a tree. He didn't recognize Paul David Hewson's name, but he figured there was a good chance it might be written on one of the outfits in the Wardrobe Studio.

He burst into the cabin and was about to start looking through the shirts when a stern voice stopped him in his tracks.

"Stop right there!"

He turned and saw Lorraine sitting at a table.

"You do *not* come into this cabin without wiping off your shoes."

He looked down and realized that his right shoe was still caked with mud from his puddle encounter.

"Sorry," he said sheepishly as he went outside and wiped his shoes on the welcome mat.

He stepped back in and one at a time showed her the soles of both shoes.

"Better," she said. "Now what do you want?"

"Paul David Hewson's sleeve," he said. "It's my clue."

Lorraine cocked her head to one side as

she mentally went through the wardrobe inventory. "We don't have it," she finally said, shaking her head.

His shoulders drooped a little bit. "What do you mean?"

"I mean I've been organizing this wardrobe all summer. Nothing in here belongs to anyone with the name Paul David Hewson."

"Can I check?" he asked, "just to be sure."

"Let me see your hands," she joked.

He held them up, and they were spotless.

"Okay," she said with a smile. "Have fun."

"So what are you doing here?" he asked as he began searching the first rack of clothes. "Is this where your clue led you?"

"My clue isn't really much of a clue," she said as she held up a pillowcase that made a loud, clinking noise. "It's more of a chore."

"What's in there?" Colby asked.

"Keys," she told him. "Lots and lots of keys."

She held the pillowcase open and poured the keys out on the table.

"Did Brown give you a poem?" Colby asked.

"Yes, he did," she answered, pushing a stray strand of red hair out of her eyes. She held up a piece of paper. The poem was called "A Glam-Rock Costume for Lorraine."

"Nice title," he said.

She started reading it:

"Queen and ELTON knew how to dress
When they wanted to impress.
And you can, too, if you please—
Just solve the riddle of these KEYS."

Colby laughed. "Brown really got into the whole mysterious-poetry thing, didn't he?"

"Apparently," she said. "So I've been lugging this pillowcase around and trying each and every key in any lock I can find. Right now I'm trying this file cabinet."

"Have you had any luck so far?"

"Of course not," she said with a laugh.

"It's frustrating, but it is kind of fun."

"Especially when you consider that we might actually get to perform with a piece of rock-and-roll history," he added. "That would be too cool."

For a moment they stopped and looked at each other. Camp Rock had exceeded their wildest expectations, and this was the icing on the cake.

"Can you believe any of this?" Lorraine asked.

"No," Colby said. "It's beyond incredible."

"Incredible," she repeated.

As much as she wanted to stop and just enjoy the moment, she had a mystery to solve. One by one, Lorraine started trying the keys in the locked file cabinet. Most didn't fit at all, although a couple slid in. None, however, unlocked the cabinet.

Meanwhile, Colby went through the racks and racks of clothing. And, like Lorraine, he looked for a sign that he was on the right track. Every costume had a tag on it, and he checked the front and back of each one looking for anything about Paul David Hewson.

Without even realizing it, he had started singing the song from the recording studio. It was the old U2 song, and pretty soon Lorraine started singing along with him. They both liked the song, but more importantly they both could relate to what it was saying—they were still no closer to finding what they were looking for.

CHAPTER SIX

Tess Tyler had a secret.

She had spent much of the past two days grumbling about having to clean bathrooms and cabins. After all, that's what everyone expected. But the truth was, she could have easily avoided it all. Her mother had arranged for a limo to come to camp and pick her up after the Parents Concert, but Tess canceled it.

Even though she tried to act as if she was above it all, Tess loved being at Camp Rock. She would much rather hang out with the other five and clean up the camp than go home and sit around her big, empty house while her mother was on the road touring.

Even though she wasn't always good at showing it, these were the best friends she had. She only wished her other cabinmates, Ella Pador and Peggy Dupree, had been able to stay on, too.

She was also thrilled with the musical mysteries, although she wasn't having any luck solving hers, either. She was sitting in the camp library staring at the contents of her envelope—a poem and an iPod.

She slipped on the headphones and pressed PLAY. There were nine songs on the playlist and each was by a harmonica player named Eivets Rednow. She actually liked the music, but had never heard of anyone named Eivets.

To make things more confusing, on the

back of the player there was a note that said, *Stressed Reward.*

"I'm stressed all right," she said. "So where's my reward?"

She read the poem, but that wasn't much help either.

> *If you want to find that Motown sound*
> *You've got to turn the beat around.*
> *Add only notes that are choice*
> *And sing them with Aretha's voice.*

She figured that "Aretha" had to have something to do with Aretha Franklin, the Queen of Soul. But there was nothing in the poem that helped her. She listened to the Eivets Rednow songs, hoping that something would click and put her on the right track.

Sitting across from Tess was Mitchie. She wasn't doing any better. Mitchie had read and reread her clue at least twenty times. Each time she hoped she'd notice something that she had missed before. But the clue just continued to baffle her. Like the others, her envelope contained a poem.

The secret of the new-wave sound
Is out there waiting to be found.
Follow the groups, 'cause it's a fact
This clue has no solo act.

When she got frustrated trying to figure that out, she moved to the other sheet of paper that was in her envelope. It was even harder to understand than the poem.

To Mitchie, it looked like a page from a baby-name book. Except for a few scattered words in bold, all it had was a long list of names:

Phil, Tony, Mike **BY** Jack, Eric, Ginger **AND** Anthony, John, Michael, Chad. Belinda, Jane, Charlotte, Kathy, Gina, **OUT** Jim, John, Ray, Robby. Neal, Ross, Jonathan, Steve, **TO** Renaldo, Abdul, Lawrence, Levi **NEAR** Don,

Glenn, Don, Bernie, Randy, Timothy, Joe, **NEST. WHERE** Phillip, Larry, Johnny, Ralph, Al, Maurice, Verdine, Andrew **MEET. LOOK UNDER** James, Tommy, Todd, Lawrence, Ricky, Dennis.

At first, she wondered if maybe the names corresponded to campers and what cabins they were in. There had been two boys named Anthony and Michael who were in the same cabin. And there had also been a Jane, a Kathy, and a Charlotte. But they had all been in different cabins.

When she couldn't make that work, she tried to make a sentence out of the words that weren't names. That didn't work either. So she just sat there thinking and thinking, trying to crack the code.

She looked at Tess, and the two of them shook their heads.

Like Tess and Mitchie, Shane was frustrated and confused. But, unlike them, he was also getting hot and tired. That's because he was digging holes in the ground.

He had taken Brown's map and the shovel from his porch and followed his clue out to the edge of the camp. He read it again to make sure he had it right.

You need to Let It Be
If you want to stay on track.
Take the Long and Winding Road,
Then Dig It and Get Back.

He thought he had done everything the clue said. There was only one long and winding road at the camp. It was a trail that ran right from Brown's cabin and headed out around the lake.

Shane had followed the path to where it ended. That's when he started digging. He figured that if he could "dig it," he'd find the treasure and then "get back" to the camp for the show.

At least, that's what he thought at first. After digging seven holes and working up quite a sweat, he was wondering if maybe he had it all wrong. He was just about to start on hole number eight when he heard a clanging. It was Mrs. Torres ringing everybody in for lunch.

"Saved by the bell," he said with a tired sigh. He picked up the shovel and started the long walk back to the center of camp. Along the way he kept a lookout for any signs or hints but saw none.

Shane was the last one to make it back to the mess hall and when he saw the other campers' faces, he knew in an instant that none of them had been successful in finding their artifacts either. There was a general sense of frustration around the table. This was despite the fact that Mrs. Torres had made one of her most popular meals—spicy chicken quesadillas with pico de gallo and guacamole.

"I think I have tried these keys in half the

locks in the entire camp," Lorraine moaned. "And not one even came close to opening."

"I've looked through more clothing today than I have in my entire life. Nothing helped," Colby said, taking a bite of his lunch. "Although this quesadilla is delicious."

"Did anyone come even close to figuring out what they were supposed to be looking for?" Caitlyn asked.

They all shook their heads.

"Not at all," Mitchie said sadly. "I can't even figure out how to read my clue."

"Maybe it's all a big prank," Tess offered. "Maybe there is no real way to solve the mysteries. Maybe it's Brown's way of putting one over on us on the very last day."

"It's not a prank," a voice said.

They turned and saw Brown walking toward them. "I warned you that it would be hard," he said, smiling. "But don't you see— that's what will make it great when you solve the clues."

Lorraine laughed. "*If* we solve them."

"You will," he said. "I have faith in you. Remember what I told you about the Beach Boys and how they got their sound. Be like the Beach Boys."

He took a tortilla chip and dipped it in the guacamole. "Delicious," he said. "I will miss you all. But I will especially miss Connie's amazing guacamole dip." He dipped another chip, took a bite, and smiled.

"Good luck, everyone! Remember, be like the Beach Boys." He took one more chip and left.

Once he was gone, Colby turned to the others. "Now I'm even more confused. What did he tell us about the Beach Boys that's a clue?"

"You've got me," Caitlyn said.

Mitchie thought back over the conversation. "It's how the Beach Boys got their sound. What did he tell us about that?"

"It was the harmony," Shane said. "How

the five of them came together to make one sound."

"You're right," Tess responded. "That's what he said. But how does that relate to us? Are we supposed to sing together?"

"Maybe we're supposed to solve the puzzles . . . together," Colby said, his eyes growing wide as the thought struck him. "Work as a team."

Mitchie nodded. "I think you may be right. Maybe that will help us."

"Right," Caitlyn said. "Like if we split all the keys up, we can try more locks faster."

"It's worth a try," Shane said. "Let's see them."

Lorraine took her pillowcase full of keys and dumped the contents onto the table.

"Man, you weren't kidding," Shane said. "There must be about a hundred of them."

Something about that number caught Mitchie's attention. "Wait a second," she said, struggling to figure out what was tickling her brain. "What about the poem that went with them?"

Lorraine pulled a folded piece of paper out of her pocket. She opened it up and read to them, "A Glam-Rock Costume for Lorraine, by Brown Cesario."

"Queen and ELTON knew how to dress
When they wanted to impress.
And you can, too, if you please—
Just solve the riddle of these KEYS."

She set the paper down on the table and the group looked at it. "Notice how ELTON and KEYS are written in all capital letters," Lorraine said.

"Elton John?" Caitlyn guessed.

"It's gotta be," Lorraine said, shrugging.

Suddenly, Mitchie smiled. That was it! "Count the keys! Everyone count keys!"

They each grabbed some of the keys and started counting. When they were done they added them all up.

"Eighty-eight keys," Mitchie said.

Lorraine shook her head, realization dawning. "*Just like a piano*. There are eighty-eight keys on a piano, and there are eighty-eight keys in that pillowcase. They aren't to open a lock. They represent a piano!"

The campers didn't waste any time. They made a mad dash outside and downstairs to the B-Note. The camp's snack bar and hang-out was conveniently located right below the mess hall. In the corner of the room was an upright piano. When they got there they found a piece of sheet music.

Lorraine rushed over and looked at it. "It's an Elton John song!"

Now they were all getting excited.

"Play it," Tess said.

Lorraine recognized it right away. She loved Elton John and played the song perfectly. Except, for some reason, one note kept coming out wrong.

"You're missing a note there," Tess said.

"No, I'm not," Lorraine said, smiling. "Something's blocking it."

Lorraine stood up, opened the top of the piano, and looked inside.

"What is it?" Mitchie asked.

"A pair of sunglasses," Lorraine said as she pulled a pair of incredibly outlandish sunglasses out of a case.

"They're not just any sunglasses," Brown said. He had slipped into the room unseen while they were all focusing on the piano. "Elton John wore those sunglasses while he was on tour back before you were born. Try them on."

"Really?" Lorraine said.

"Really," he replied.

Lorraine slipped the glasses on. "How do they look?"

"Incredible," Mitchie said. "Like they were made for you."

"Elton wore lots of ridiculous outfits and

sunglasses and costumes. Do you know why?" Brown asked.

"I read about it in one of your magazines," Lorraine said. "Unlike guitar players who got to dance around the stage, Elton was always stuck behind his piano. He wanted to make sure he stood out and that people remembered him. So he wore those outfits."

"Excellent," Brown said with a smile. "And tonight, when you're playing piano, you're going to be wearing the same glasses and you're going to stand out, too."

The others all shared a look. Now that they had some success, they were ready to tackle the rest of the mysteries—together.

CHAPTER
SEVEN

"**W**hich mystery should we solve next?" Lorraine asked.

"How about Caitlyn's?" Tess said.

"Let's do it," Shane said, impressed that Tess was thinking about somebody other than herself. "What do you have, Caitlyn?"

"Here's what was in my envelope," she said, holding up the sheet music. "There are scales, and the word *produce* is written across the top."

"What do scales have to do with rap?" Tess asked.

"And how do you 'produce' them?" Caitlyn said.

"Maybe if you recorded it and then you gave it a hip-hop beat," added Shane.

"Or maybe," Colby said, getting into it, "instead of an instrument, one of us should do it like a human beat box? That would be kind of like rap."

"All these are good ideas," Caitlyn said. "Better than anything I came up with."

"Can I see the poem?" Tess asked.

Caitlyn handed it to her, and Tess read it to everyone else. "Recipe for Rap," she said.

"A producer is a special fixer,
An artist who controls the mixer
To blend the parts to make them cook
And bake a sound that's off the hook."

They all just sat there and thought about

the poem for a minute. Tess passed it around, and they each took a look. Nothing was coming to them.

While they were thinking, Colby started looking through the canteen's cabinets.

"You think the clue is there?" Caitlyn asked.

"I'm not looking for a clue," he said. "I'm looking for food."

"Again?" Caitlyn asked.

"There isn't any," Mitchie said. "We cleaned out practically everything."

Shane laughed and looked at him. "Didn't you just eat lunch?"

"Yeah, I did," Colby said. "But food helps me think. Besides, that poem got me hungry with all the talk of cooking and baking and blenders and mixers."

Tess smiled. "Colby, you're a genius. Let me see that again."

Caitlyn handed her the poem.

"Listen to the words that are in this," she

said. "Recipe, mixer, blend, cook, bake. That can't just be a coincidence."

Mitchie couldn't help noticing that Tess was being really helpful and nice. With a pang, she realized she was going to miss Tess—attitude or not. "You're right," she said, snapping out of it. "We better go to the kitchen."

In a flash, they all bolted out the door of the B-Note and headed back upstairs. When they walked into the kitchen, they were greeted by the delicious smell of the dessert that Connie was baking.

"I'm back in heaven," Colby said, savoring the aroma. "Just the smell of food is helping me think better."

"Good," Mitchie said. "Because I'm still stumped. Caitlyn and I have gone over every inch of this kitchen and we didn't see anything that looked like it belonged in the Rock and Roll Hall of Fame."

Shane looked to Connie, who was checking

the oven. "I don't suppose you can help us at all."

"Sorry. I'm not supposed to give any hints."

"Okay," Colby said. "I know you guys think I'm a food crazy. But am I the only one who thinks that smells absolutely delicious?"

"It does smell pretty incredible," Shane agreed.

"Are you allowed to tell us what you're cooking?" Colby asked Mrs. Torres.

"Of course I am," she said with a smile. "Apple Brown Betty."

"It even *sounds* delicious. Can you tell us what's in it?"

Mitchie rolled her eyes.

Connie laughed. "Bread, butter, sugar, cinnamon, and *two pounds of apples*."

"Wait a second," Mitchie said. "Why'd you change your voice when you said *two pounds of apples*?"

"Did I?" her mom said with a sly smile. "I better get out of here before I get in trouble."

"She's trying to help us out," Mitchie said when her mom was gone. "*Two pounds of apples* is a hint."

"I've got it!" Colby exclaimed.

The others all turned to him excitedly.

"You do?"

"It's the cinnamon," he said.

Shane gave him a perplexed look. "What's the cinnamon?"

"The smell that's driving me crazy," he said. "I *love* the smell of cinnamon."

Caitlyn took a deep breath. "We're trying to focus here," she said through clenched teeth. "Can you forget about the food and think about the clues?"

"Sorry," he said with a gulp. He knew not to mess with Caitlyn when she was on a mission.

They thought for a moment.

"I've got it!" Colby cried again. "It's the apples."

"That's it," Caitlyn said, getting truly

frustrated. "Forget about the food."

"No," he said. "This time I was talking about the clues. I figured out the hint."

"You did?" Tess said. "What is it?"

"Measure out two pounds of apples," he said.

Shane gave him a look. "Is this some elaborate plan to get an extra serving of Apple Brown Betty?"

"Just do it."

Shane grabbed some apples and put them on the kitchen scale until it read two pounds.

"Now what?" he said.

"How did you weigh them?" Colby asked.

"On the scale." Now Shane was getting frustrated.

"Not just any scale," Colby laughed. "It's specially made to weigh fruits and vegetables. It's called a *produce scale.*"

"That's right," Mitchie said. "A produce scale. The clue isn't to produce scales. It's to check the *produce* scale."

Caitlyn gave Colby a big smile and tossed him an apple to eat. She lifted the bottom of the scale. Underneath was a key.

"Ugh," Lorraine said. "Another key."

"Except this time, I know exactly where *that* key goes," Mitchie said. "*That's* the key to my mom's catering truck."

They went out back and unlocked the door to Connie's catering truck. Everything was neatly put away, just as they had left it. They looked at the drawers, all clearly labeled.

"Now what?" Caitlyn asked.

Colby noticed a drawer marked DESSERTS.

"Ooh," he said. "Can we look in here?"

He reached for the drawer, but Mitchie playfully smacked his hand. "No."

Colby pulled it back and took a whiff, wondering if he could smell any of the desserts.

"I think I know," Tess said, ignoring Colby and his insatiable appetite. "What's the key piece of equipment for producing rap music?"

"A mixer," Caitlyn said.

Tess turned to the wall full of compartments, each one specially marked to hold a particular item. She pointed at one.

Caitlyn smiled and opened the compartment. Inside was a mixer. But it wasn't a kitchen mixer. It was a recording mixer.

Caitlyn pulled it out as if it were a priceless antique.

"Kind of basic, isn't it?" Colby said.

"Yeah," Caitlyn said softly. It had to be at least twenty-five years old. "The mixers we have in our studios are ten times more advanced. But this one's a classic."

She turned it over and on the bottom was a piece of masking tape. Written across the tape in big black letters was the name RUN-DMC.

Caitlyn nearly fainted. "I don't believe it! This mixer was used by Run-DMC. They were legendary in the early days of rap."

The group stood quietly in the back of

Connie's catering truck and let Caitlyn enjoy the moment.

"Brown Cesario is the coolest person ever!" she announced. She held the mixer to her chest, almost reverently. "What are we finding next?"

She scanned the room, and Colby raised his hand.

"Anyone know anything about Paul David Hewson and his sleeve?" he asked.

"I don't know anything about his sleeve," Mitchie said. "But I know who he is."

"So do I," Tess commented. She and Mitchie shared a smile while Colby started bouncing up and down.

"How do you know Paul David Hewson?!" Colby pleaded.

"Everyone here knows him," Tess said.

"If *I* knew," he said a little crossly, "I wouldn't be this desperate."

"I bet you a candy bar that you know at least five songs by him," Mitchie said.

"Probably ten!" Tess added.

"You've got a candy bar?" he asked. "Is it in the desserts drawer?"

"No!" Mitchie said, laughing. "Forget about the desserts drawer." She slyly popped open the door to the minifridge in the back of the truck. She pulled out a king-size candy bar.

"Is that frozen?" Colby asked, desperate to take a bite. "They're so good frozen."

"Frozen solid," Mitchie told him. "I'm going to give you a hint and let you have a chance to earn this."

"Okay. Give me the hint."

"If you watched Music Makers on *Hot Tunes* as much as Tess and I do, you'd already have figured this out," she said. "Paul David Hewson is his real name, but you know him by his stage name."

Colby racked his brain for a moment. He thought about the clue. It was the sheet music from the U2 song, "I Still Haven't

Found What I'm Looking For." That's when it hit him.

"Does it have something to do with U2?" he asked.

Mitchie dangled the candy bar ever so closely in front of him.

"Is Paul David Hewson's stage name Bono?"

Mitchie tossed him the candy bar. "You are correct, sir."

"Excellent," Colby said as he quickly unwrapped the candy bar and took a bite. "Now we know it has something to do with Bono. But that still doesn't solve the problem. What's hidden up his sleeve? I've been through the entire Wardrobe Studio and there was nothing that belonged to Bono."

"He's right," Lorraine said. "I think I would have noticed that item myself."

Shane smiled and nodded as he remembered something. "Earlier, when my uncle played the Beach Boys album? What did he call that thing that held the record?"

"The sleeve!" they all said in unison.

"It's hidden in a U2 album!" Colby cried.

They rushed out of the catering truck and ran to Brown's cabin. He was sitting in his chair, hiding his face behind a newspaper. He knew exactly why they were there.

"Careful with my records," he warned them.

They all stepped back and let Colby carefully flip through the albums. Luckily, Brown was organized, and the records were alphabetized so U2 was easy to find. Colby randomly pulled out an album. Nothing. Then he pulled out another and removed the record sleeve. A picture fell out of the sleeve and onto the floor. He picked it up. It was a picture of the band, and there was a note attached to it. He read the note to everyone.

"Turn around and you will finally have found what you're looking for."

When Colby turned around, Brown lowered

the newspaper to reveal that he was wearing a black cowboy hat. Colby looked down at the picture of the band.

"Wait a second," Colby said, putting it all together. "That hat looks just like Bono's hat."

"It doesn't just *look* like it," Brown said.

"Are you serious?" Lorraine blurted out. "That's *Bono's* cowboy hat?"

"No, it's my cowboy hat," he said with a laugh. "But it used to be his. I tell you, that man is an amazing singer but a terrible poker player."

Brown took off the hat and handed it to Colby.

"Take good care of that."

"Yeah," Lorraine said. "Chocolate and superstar memorabilia simply do not mix."

Colby nodded and carefully placed the hat on his head. Suddenly, he felt just like a rock star.

CHAPTER EIGHT

So far, the campers had found three of the six pieces of memorabilia. They were already halfway there and still had a few hours left until the concert was scheduled to start.

"You know, we just might make it," Mitchie said excitedly. "Tess, let's solve yours next."

Tess smiled. "Are you sure?"

"I'm positive," Mitchie said with a firm nod. "Show us what you've got."

Tess reached into her envelope and pulled out her poem. Clearing her throat, she read it aloud:

"If you want to find that Motown sound,
You've got to turn the beat around.
Add only notes that are choice
And sing them with Aretha's voice."

When she was done, Tess looked around at the others to see if they had any ideas.

She was met with blank stares. Apparently, they didn't.

"This was in the envelope, too," she said as she pulled out the iPod. "It only has nine songs on it, all of them by an artist named Eivets Rednow."

"Seriously?" Colby said.

"See for yourself," she said, handing the iPod to him.

"What kind of name is Eivets?" Caitlyn asked.

"What era are you supposed to be again?" Shane asked.

"Soul. Rhythm and blues. The whole Motown sound."

Lorraine noticed the note on the back of the iPod. "What's that say?"

"You're going to love this," Tess answered. "It just says *Stressed Reward*."

"Stressed reward?" Lorraine repeated. "What's that mean?"

Tess laughed. "That's what I've been trying to figure out all day."

"This is some good stuff," Colby said, a little too loudly. He was wearing the headphones and jamming out to the music, so he had no sense of volume. "Eivets is an incredible harmonica player."

Mitchie looked around the room and locked on to Brown's record collection. It was huge and filled an entire wall. "Brown has a lot of albums. I wonder if he has any by Mr. Rednow."

Shane thought that was a pretty good idea. "Let's check it out. Would it be under *E* for *Eivets* or *R* for *Rednow*?"

"Check both," she said.

"Be careful with my records," Brown called from the other room where he had gone in order to be out of their way.

"I *am* being careful, Uncle Brown," Shane answered, rolling his eyes good-naturedly.

Mitchie smiled. She knew just how it felt to have a relative at camp looking over your shoulder.

Shane quickly scanned the *E*'s and found Eivets Rednow right between the Eagles and Elvis.

"Here it is," Shane said as he pulled the album from the shelf. He brought it over to the table and set it down.

"We're *still* being careful," Shane called out to his uncle as he handed it to Mitchie.

"Thank you," Brown said.

The album cover didn't give them much

help. It just had a picture of a drum set. The name Eivets Rednow was written across the top.

"Well at least we know what his drums look like," Lorraine said. "I only wish that helped us somehow."

Caitlyn flipped it over and looked at the back. "There's not even a picture of him. Who does that? It's like he's purposely trying to keep us from figuring out who he is."

She set the album back down. Colby was still wearing headphones and rocking out to the harmonica music. "What about the sleeve?" he said. "Should we check that?"

He slid the sleeve out of the cover and looked at it while the others tried to think of a new direction to follow. Suddenly something caught Colby's eye, and he leaned in close for a better look.

"Too funny," he said with a laugh.

"What?" Tess asked.

"Listen to what it says here in tiny print

across the top corner of the sleeve." He read it to them. "'How do you spell Stevie Wonder backward?'"

"What?" Mitchie asked him.

"That's what it says right here." He held it up for them to see.

"How do you spell Stevie Wonder backward," Tess said, finally understanding it. "Eivets Rednow is Stevie Wonder spelled backward!"

It took the others a moment to run through it in their heads, but when they did they realized she was exactly right.

"Unbelievable," Caitlyn said. "Why did he do that? Why did he release an album with his name spelled backward?"

"Would you like me to tell you?" Brown called from the other room.

"Please!" Caitlyn cried.

Brown entered the room and smiled. "Stevie Wonder was a big star who loved to play the harmonica so much he wanted to release a harmonica album. But his record label, Motown, didn't want to confuse his fans by releasing an album without him singing on it. So they flipped his name around and released it that way."

"That's what it means in the poem when you say that in order to get the Motown sound, you've got to turn the beat around," Tess exclaimed. "You've got to turn his name around."

"Exactly." Brown nodded.

"We have to go back to the catering truck," Colby suddenly said.

"We do?" Shane asked, raising an eyebrow.

"Yes, we do."

Colby looked at Brown who flashed a congratulatory smile. "Well done, Colby," he said, praising him. "I was worried no one would get that one."

"What one?" Lorraine pleaded.

"Just follow me," Colby said. "It will all become clear."

When they got to the catering truck, all eyes turned to Colby. He had remained smugly silent for the entire walk.

"Okay," Tess said when they arrived, "why are we here?"

"Stressed Reward!" Colby answered, as if that would make it all instantly clear.

He let them think about it for a moment, but no one seemed to understand what he was getting at.

"Do the same trick to it that Motown did to Stevie Wonder's name," he explained.

After a few moments Mitchie figured it out. "I don't believe it. I *do not* believe it."

"You should," Colby said with a laugh. "*And*, if you hadn't slapped my hand an hour ago we would have found Tess's prize by accident."

"Do you mind telling the rest of us what you two are talking about?" Lorraine asked.

"Stressed Reward," Mitchie said. "If you

spell it backward like Eivets Rednow, it spells *Desserts Drawer*."

Caitlyn started laughing hysterically. "That is too funny. You stopped him from opening it."

"I know," Mitchie said.

Tess opened the drawer marked DESSERTS. In it was an old-style microphone and a note. She took them out and read the note aloud.

"This microphone was used in concert by Aretha Franklin in 1974." She held it for a moment and admired it. She may have been born rock royalty, but that didn't mean she didn't appreciate musical greatness. This was awe-inspiring. "You know, I'd say this pretty much makes cleaning bathrooms worth it."

"Okay, Colby. You deserve another candy bar for that," Mitchie said as she reached into the minifridge and pulled out the frozen treat. She tossed it to him. Instantly, he unwrapped it and started eating.

The catering truck was pretty crowded

with the six of them, so they went back outside and sat down at a nearby picnic table.

"Which clue do we try next?" Lorraine asked.

"Both," Caitlyn said. "We've got a lot of brainpower here. Let's put the last two clues on the table and figure these suckers out."

Mitchie and Shane pulled out their clues and put them down. The others immediately began examining them.

Looking around the table, Mitchie felt a surge of happiness. When the day started, she had been worried about how it would feel when camp ended. She had been dreading this last day, but it had turned out to be so much fun. The six of them had been too busy chasing Brown's clues around camp to worry about anything or to think about endings.

The best part was that they were all

working together. There was no fighting or bickering. They weren't competing. They were just six friends having a good time.

"I think I've got something," Lorraine said, holding up Shane's clue.

"I hope it doesn't require any more digging," Shane said.

"I don't think so," she replied. She pointed down at the poem:

You need to Let It Be
If you want to stay on track.
Take The Long and Winding Road,
Then Dig It and Get Back.

"Check out the capitalization," she said. "Let It Be. The Long and Winding Road. Dig It. Get Back. They're all capitalized. Those aren't directions. Those are song titles."

Shane groaned. Suddenly it seemed so obvious. "You're absolutely right. Those are all Beatles songs."

"I think we need to pay one more visit to Brown's record collection," Tess said.

Mitchie nodded. "I think you're right." They could go back to her clue later. There was no use in slowing down their momentum while the group was on a roll.

A few minutes later, they were all walking into Brown's cabin for what felt like the umpteenth time.

"Welcome back," Brown said with a smile as the campers trudged through the door. "So happy to see you again."

"Do you mind if we look at your records one more time?" Caitlyn asked. "And we know. We'll be careful."

Brown smiled. "Go right ahead."

Shane flipped through the *B*'s until he found The Beatles. He pulled the album *Let It Be* from the shelf.

"All right," Shane said, looking at it. "I think the key is the word *track*."

"Songs are called tracks, right? Maybe

they're referring to the track numbers," Mitchie suggested.

"That's a pretty good idea," Shane said as he looked at them. "The Long and Winding Road is track ten. Dig It is track five. And Get Back is number twelve."

"Ten-five-twelve?" Mitchie said, repeating the numbers. "What does that mean?"

"It sounds like a locker combination," Colby joked.

"You know, it kind of does," said Lorraine.

Suddenly Shane's eyes grew wide. "It can't be."

"What?" Tess asked.

Shane took a deep breath and tried not to get too excited. "My uncle has one piece of music memorabilia that is so valuable to him he keeps it locked in a display case."

"What is it?" Mitchie asked, getting very excited.

"I don't even want to say it out loud," Shane said. "Let's just go check it out. I'm sure I'm wrong. Uncle Brown would never . . ." His voice trailed off as he led them into Brown's study. On the wall was a wood-and-glass display case that held an electric guitar. On the bottom of the case was a combination lock.

"Ten-five-twelve," Mitchie reminded him.

Shane took another deep breath and tried the numbers. When they were set, he pressed the release button. The case popped open.

"Uncle Brown," he said, shaking his head, "I can't play this guitar."

Brown was now standing at the door. "Oh, yes, you can," he said. "You've grown up a lot this summer. I am so proud of you. And you are more than ready to play that guitar."

"Whose guitar is it?" Tess asked.

Brown smiled. "Paul McCartney's. He gave it to me after a concert when I was first starting out."

"Why?"

For a moment, Brown's eyes grew misty, as

though he were reliving the moment. Then he shook his head and answered. "He gave it to me because he is an incredibly sweet and generous man. I think he wanted to inspire me."

Mitchie smiled. "Like you inspire all of us."

Shane wiped his palms on his pants, carefully reached up, and took out the legendary guitar. "I've got a feeling this is going to be an amazing 'think about it for the rest of your life' kind of night."

"Good," Brown said. "But don't forget, you've still got one more mystery to solve."

CHAPTER NINE

The library was completely silent. The six remaining campers were sprawled out on chairs and couches trying to figure out the final clue. Unfortunately, they had been trying for a while and were getting nowhere.

"Five out of six is not bad," Mitchie reasoned. "In fact, I think it's pretty impressive. We don't need to find all of them."

"We are not giving up," Caitlyn said. "We

have come too far to quit. You need your prize, too, just like the rest of us."

"The *far* is not the problem," said Mitchie. "It's the *long* that has me worried. As in 'we've taken too long and are running out of time.'"

"Shhh," Colby said. "We're trying to think."

Mitchie appreciated their determination, but she didn't see any solution on the horizon.

"I mean, my mom has been here all summer, but your parents will be arriving soon and they're expecting a show," she reminded everyone.

Her words fell on deaf ears. No one was listening. She flashed pleading eyes at Shane and Caitlyn, but they both shook her off. Finally, she turned to Tess.

"Reason with them, Tess," Mitchie begged. "You're a pro. You understand that the show must go on. I mean, aren't you just dying to use Aretha Franklin's microphone?"

"I am," Tess said as she looked Mitchie in the eye, "but I'm not going near that stage until we find your piece of rock-and-roll history. And that's that."

Such a strong, selfless statement coming from Tess totally caught Mitchie by surprise. She had always considered Tess completely selfish. She was beginning to realize that she had misjudged her.

"You're serious?"

"Absolutely!" Tess said.

To Mitchie this meant more than anything they might find. This meant that Tess was a true friend.

"All right, then," Mitchie said, reinvigorated. "Let's go over the clues one more time." First she read the poem:

"The secret of the new-wave sound
Is out there waiting to be found.
Follow the groups 'cause it's a fact
This clue has no solo act."

When she finished reading it, she looked around the room to see if anyone had miraculously come up with something this time around. No such luck.

"And here are the names," she said as she read the other clue aloud.

"'Phil, Tony, Mike **BY** Jack, Eric, Ginger **AND** Anthony, John, Michael, Chad. Belinda, Jane, Charlotte, Kathy, Gina, **OUT** Jim, John, Ray, Robby. Neal, Ross, Jonathan, Steve, **TO** Renaldo, Abdul, Lawrence, Levi **NEAR** Don, Glenn, Don, Bernie, Randy, Timothy, Joe, **NEST**. **WHERE** Phillip, Larry, Johnny, Ralph, Al, Maurice, Verdine, Andrew **MEET**. **LOOK UNDER** James, Tommy, Todd, Lawrence, Ricky, Dennis.'"

The silence returned, and Mitchie was about to take another pass at convincing them to quit.

"Think about all the clues Brown gave us," Caitlyn said. "They were multilayered. We must be missing something."

"He told us we should stay in character," Colby reminded them. "Maybe you need to solve it in character."

"How am I supposed to do that?" Mitchie asked.

"I don't know."

Mitchie tried to psych herself up. "Okay, how would the Go-Go's solve this?" she asked. "What would Linda Carlisle do."

"It's not Linda," Shane said, reminding her of the conversation that morning with her mom. "It's *Be*linda."

"That's right, I always mess that one up," Mitchie said. "What would *Be*linda Carlisle do?"

"Who's Belinda Carlisle?" Colby asked.

Mitchie struck her new-wave pose and twirled her hair around her finger. "Belinda is the lead singer of the Go-Go's."

"Belinda is also one of the names on the list," Colby said as he picked up the paper. He stabbed it with his finger. "It's right here, next to Jane, Charlotte, Kathy, and Gina."

"Unbelievable," Tess said, totally frustrated that she hadn't thought of this earlier. "When were the Go-Go's at the top?" she asked Mitchie.

"Early to mid-eighties."

Tess got up and walked over to the magazine rack. It contained old issues Brown had collected over the years. She pulled out a *Rolling Stone* from 1984. The Go-Go's were on the cover. She flipped through the magazine until she found the article about them and read the caption under their picture.

"Belinda, Jane, Charlotte, Kathy, and Gina. Those are the first names of the women in the band." She held the magazine up for them to see. Then she pointed at the clue. "These are all names of band members."

"'Follow the groups 'cause it's a fact,'" Lorraine read from the poem. "'This clue has no solo act.'"

Using the books and magazines in the

library, the six of them went about the somewhat slow process of finding bands that corresponded with the people on the list. As they did, Mitchie replaced the names of the people with the names of the bands.

When they were finished the clue read:

"**Genesis** by **Cream** and **Red Hot Chili Peppers**. **Go-Go** out **The Doors**. **Journey** to **Four Tops** near **Eagles** nest. Where **Earth, Wind and Fire** meet. Look under **Styx**."

"It's like a treasure map," Mitchie said. "If we follow the band names, they'll tell us where to go."

They broke the directions down step by step.

"The first one is: 'Genesis by Cream and Red Hot Chili Peppers,'" Tess said.

"Genesis means beginning," Shane said. "So the beginning is somewhere where there is cream and red hot chili peppers."

"The kitchen," Lorraine and Caitlyn blurted out at the same time.

"This might just work," Mitchie said, getting more excited.

They all trooped to the kitchen once more.

"What's next?" Shane asked.

"'Go-Go out the Doors,'" Mitchie said.

"Okay," Shane said. He smiled. "Out the doors we go."

The six of them walked out the double doors that led toward the lake. When they were outside, Mitchie read the next step.

"'Journey to Four Tops near Eagles nest.'"

They thought about it for a moment and looked around the camp.

"There," Shane said, pointing across the lake. "The picnic pavilion has four tops, like a sand castle."

"And it's right by that eagle's nest," Colby added, pointing to a small island in the middle of the lake. "We've got to go there."

It was getting late, and their families were due to arrive at any moment. But the group didn't care. They were on a mission. Together they hurried down to the dock, hopped into a pair of canoes, and started paddling. They were on an actual treasure hunt, and it was thrilling.

"Can you believe this?" Mitchie exclaimed, paddling as fast as she could.

"No, I can't," Shane answered from his spot in the back.

Mitchie smiled at where the day had brought them. It felt right to be out on the water one last time with Shane. She had so many fond memories of taking canoe rides with him. But this ride was like no other.

They were all panting and short of breath by the time they had reached the island and pulled the canoes up onto the shore.

"What's the next clue?" Tess asked excitedly.

"'Where Earth, Wind and Fire meet. Look under Styx.'"

Mitchie figured this one out.

The camp was old, and years ago there had

been a caretaker's cabin on the island. The cabin was gone, but its brick chimney was still standing. Brown had taken them there for bonfires a few times over the summer.

"The chimney," Mitchie said. "That's where Earth, Wind and Fire meet."

The others nodded and smiled. They were getting really close. They hiked down the trail to the chimney.

"Now 'look under Styx,'" Mitchie said, reading the last step in the directions.

Next to the chimney was a pile of kindling sticks that Brown used when he started the bonfires. Mitchie kneeled down and pushed the sticks aside.

"What's under there?" Caitlyn asked.

"I don't know," Mitchie said. "I only see bricks."

"Bricks?"

Mitchie looked at them for a moment and noticed something. There was writing on the side of each brick.

"The bricks have names on them," she said.

"Names of bands?" asked Lorraine.

"Singers?" said Colby.

"No," Mitchie replied. "Each brick has one of our names on it."

This caught them all by surprise.

"I think that means they're for us. We better dig them up and bring them back to camp," Caitlyn said.

Shane slumped and let out a groan. "This is what the shovel was for. Too bad I left it back on Brown's porch."

Mitchie laughed, and they started digging the bricks out with their hands.

"We better hurry up," she said. "It's almost time for the concert to start."

By the time they had dug up the bricks and paddled back across the lake, the parents had already arrived. Shane's family couldn't make it, but he had a good substitute. His bandmates, Nate and Jason, had arrived in their tour bus. The band would be heading out to play a few end-of-summer gigs, but Nate and Jason hadn't wanted Shane to miss out on this last event. They would leave right after.

Caitlyn beamed when she saw the family RV in the dirt parking lot. "They made it," she exclaimed happily.

Mitchie's father had arrived unexpectedly to surprise her. He greeted her with a huge hug. Then she introduced him to her friends.

Brown and Dee were giving a quick tour to Lorraine's parents, and Connie was giving Colby's father a container of Apple Brown Betty for the road.

"Trust me," she said. "This will come in handy if Colby gets cranky on the trip home."

"Look who finally showed up," Brown said when the six of them reached the theater. "Are we going to be able to squeeze this show in?"

"Definitely," Mitchie said. "But first, will you explain the bricks."

Brown nodded. "Those bricks used to be part of a wall at the Fillmore. That was the premiere concert venue in San Francisco. Every act played the Fillmore. All the people we've talked about today—any classic rock band you can think of—played the Fillmore.

"And during all those concerts, their music echoed off the walls. Off these bricks. Think of the incredible music that these six bricks have absorbed."

Mitchie got goosebumps and looked in wonder at the object in her hand.

"But how are we supposed to use them?" Shane asked.

"Tonight, during the show," Brown said. "We're going to line them up on the stage. That means your music is going to bounce off the same bricks. Your sounds are going to blend in with the sounds of all those amazing groups. And when you go home, you're each going to take one of the bricks with you."

"Wow!" Mitchie said. "That is so amazing."

True, she didn't have a unique piece of history to perform with tonight like the others, but this was more meaningful. This she would cherish forever.

"Of course, that will only happen if you all get onstage and perform," Brown added.

"Okay, okay. We're going."

Just then a limousine pulled up. The back door opened and T. J. Tyler sprang out. She was all alone. There was no entourage. There were no photographers. There was just Tess's mother.

"Did I miss it?" T. J. asked. "Am I too late?"

"No," Tess said, beaming. "You're right on time."

CHAPTER TEN

For as long as she could remember, Mitchie Torres dreamed of being a performing artist like the ones she saw on *Hot Tunes*. And for as long as she could remember, that dream seemed like a far-fetched idea. But now, at least for one night, she was *just* like them.

She was dressed like one of the Go-Go's and singing with someone wearing Bono's hat. Her best friend was mixing the concert on the same equipment that Jam Master Jay used to mix Run-DMC's records, and one of her newest friends was singing into Aretha Franklin's microphone. And to top it all off, the boy of her dreams was winking at her while he played Paul McCartney's guitar. Even Nate and Jason had gotten into the act and were providing backup vocals.

There may have been only a dozen or so people in the audience, but it didn't matter. To Mitchie it felt as if she were playing with all the great acts that had ever played before a full house at the Fillmore or any other rock venue.

Although Brown had thought they would each perform solo, the six campers had another plan. They told Brown they wanted to spend the concert performing as a group, blending their styles and personalities and giving the summer a proper ending.

Lorraine brought the house down when she walked onstage wearing platform boots, a sequined jumpsuit, and Elton John's sunglasses. And Mitchie's mom surprised everyone when she came out of the audience and joined them on the Go-Go's hit song, "We Got the Beat."

When Mitchie held that final note and the music faded, everyone in the crowd jumped to their feet and gave them a standing ovation. Leading the way was Brown Cesario. He had wanted to give them a memory to inspire them, and he had achieved that—and so much more.

And in return, they wanted to give him something.

"We have one more song we'd like to play," Mitchie said into the microphone. "That is if Dee was able to find the music for us."

"I've got it," a voice called out.

From the back of the auditorium, Dee came running up with a stack of sheet music. She handed it to Mitchie, who then passed it out among the others.

Lorraine was at the piano and Shane and Colby were on guitar while Tess and Mitchie shared Aretha's microphone. Even though one was wearing a blinding array of eighties colors and the other was in an elegant black-and-white gown, they somehow fit together perfectly.

Shane leaned into a microphone and said, "This one's for all the kids sitting in their rooms, listening to music and dreaming big."

He counted out a beat, and Colby started playing a bass line. Soon they were all going, all five of them singing, while Caitlyn worked the mixing board. All five of their voices came together in perfect harmony. All different eras of rock and roll combined to make one beautiful sound.

They sang the Beach Boys tune that Brown had listened to thousands of times when he was growing up. The song that had hooked him on rock and roll.

At one point in the middle of singing and

playing and dancing, Mitchie looked toward the front row where she saw Brown. His eyes were closed as he traveled back in time listening to the song.

And though it was hard to see past the stage lights, Mitchie was pretty sure she saw some tears rolling down his cheeks.

That was when Mitchie stopped worrying.

She knew that she didn't have to wonder what would happen now that Camp Rock was over. The camp was only what brought them together. It wasn't what held them together. They didn't need to be sleeping in cabins and taking classes together. They were connected by something much more important. Something that wasn't going to end when they headed home.

They were connected by the music, and that would *always* keep playing.